1.5
orange

E.R. HATHAWAY SCHOOL
256 COURT ST.
NEW BEDFORD, MA 02740

Clifford's
THANKSGIVING VISIT

NORMAN BRIDWELL

SCHOLASTIC INC.

New York Toronto London Auckland Sydney

For Alexa, Caroline, and Allison Merz

ISBN 0-590-46987-8

Copyright © 1993 by Norman Bridwell.
All rights reserved. Published by Scholastic Inc.
CLIFFORD THE BIG RED DOG® and PAWPRINT® are registered trademarks of Norman Bridwell.

12 11   7 8/9

Printed in the U.S.A.   24

First Scholastic printing, October 1993

Special thanks to R.H. Macy, Inc.
and the Macy's Thanksgiving Day Parade.

Hi! My name is Emily Elizabeth.
My dog Clifford and I have a lot of fun on Halloween.
Then, as soon as Halloween is over, we
start looking forward to Thanksgiving.

Last Thanksgiving my family flew away to visit
my grandma. Clifford had to stay home.
Our neighbors took care of him.

They were very kind, but Clifford got lonely.
He thought about his own family —
his father, his sisters, Bonnie and Claudia,
his brother, Nero. They all live in different places.

Most of all Clifford thought about his mom.
He decided to spend Thanksgiving with her.
She lives in the city.

Early Thanksgiving morning, Clifford started out.
It was easy. There weren't many cars.

But as he got near the city, there were a *lot* of cars.
Everybody seemed to be going to see their moms.

Some drivers were in a hurry.
They bumped into Clifford and honked at him.

Clifford came to a bridge. There were no cars on it.
They had all stopped. Clifford wondered why.

Soon he found out. It was a drawbridge!
And it was opening right under Clifford!

Clifford was wet and cold.

He didn't want to get back on the highway.

There was only one other way to go.

The tunnel was dark and narrow. Suddenly there was
a roar and a bright light in Clifford's eyes.

The train stopped. The people inside were
as surprised as Clifford was.

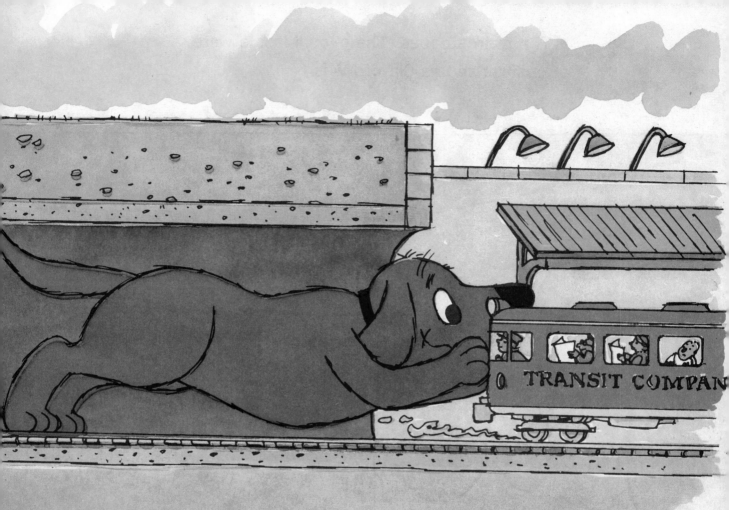

He couldn't turn around, so he pushed
the train back to the station.

Then he jumped up to the street.

He was in a strange neighborhood.
Nothing looked familiar.
Where was his mom?

Clifford saw a very tall building.
He climbed up to look around.

He could see his old neighborhood!
He could see his mom's home!
He jumped down and started walking.

A Thanksgiving Day parade was blocking his way.
Clifford usually likes parades...

... but he was in a hurry to get to his mom.
He decided to take a shortcut through the park.

He was almost there.
He passed some kids playing football in the park.

Clifford didn't mean to,
but he wound up in the game.

At last, he found his mom.

She was happy to see her little boy.

Her owner was happy, too.
He served them a nice Thanksgiving dinner.

I was having fun at grandma's house,
but I kept thinking about Clifford.
I wondered if he was thinking of me.

He was. He loves his mom, but as soon as he could, he hurried home. So did I . . .

... because I am thankful for Clifford,
and he is thankful for me.